For William, Elza, Victor, Aris, Hector,
and all the other wildlings
STAY WILD

About This Book

The illustrations for this book were made using watercolor on 220gsm Daler Rowney paper with monoprinted details added to it. This book was edited by Andrea Spooner and designed by Véronique Lefèvre Sweet. The production was supervised by Nyamekye Waliyaya, and the production editor was Jen Graham. The text was set in Varius 1 LT Std, and the display type is hand lettered.

wild beings

Dorien Brouwers

L B

Little, Brown and Company
New York Boston

We are wild beings.
Born curious and strong,

Determined and fierce.

We feel at home in the mud,

Yet we can climb mountains
and howl with the wind.

We love to run free
and leap into flight.

Our dreams give us wings.

We wander and seek
yet know how to hide.

Exploring with all of our senses,
we track the wild things.

With wide eyes and open minds,
we can see so much more.

Following our instincts,
we create magical worlds.

And when it is time to rest,
it is just for a moment…

For we are wild beings.
Wild to the core.

Our call will never cease.

Listen…

HEAR OUR...

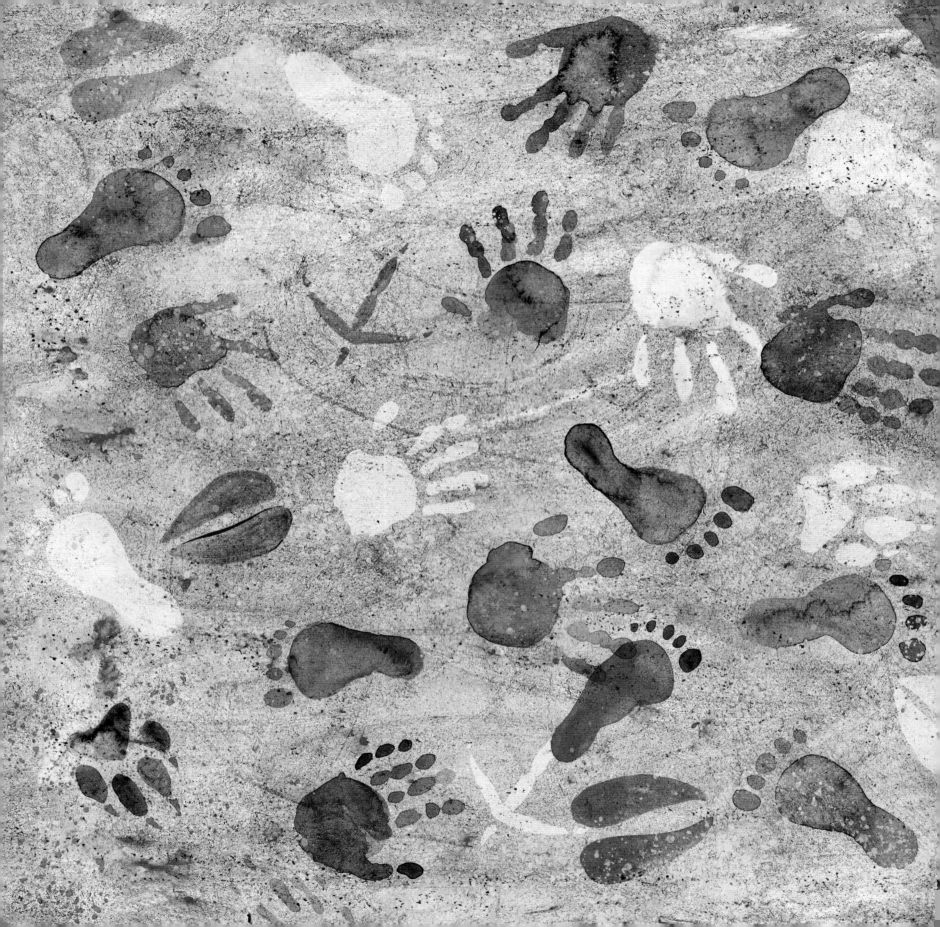